MW00960102

Adventures with The King™

A Princess PRAYER

BY
SHERI ROSE SHEPHERD

ILLUSTRATED BY
JENNIFER ZIVOIN

TYNDALE

Tyndale House Publishers, Inc.
Carol Stream, Illinois

FOCUS ON THE FAMILY®

A Princess Prayer

A Focus on the Family book published by Tyndale House Publishers, Inc., Carol Stream, Illinois 60188

Book Design by Josh Lewis
Text set in Mrs Eaves XL.

For manufacturing information regarding this product, please call 1-800-323-9400.

For information about special discounts for bulk purchases, please contact Tyndale House Publishers at csresponse@tyndale.com, or call 1-800-323-9400.

ISBN 978-1-58997-988-8

Printed in Malaysia

25 24 23 22 21 20 19
7 6 5 4 3 2 1

There once was a little girl named Elise. She wanted to be a real princess. Elise loved playing dress-up and walking down the hallway of her house.

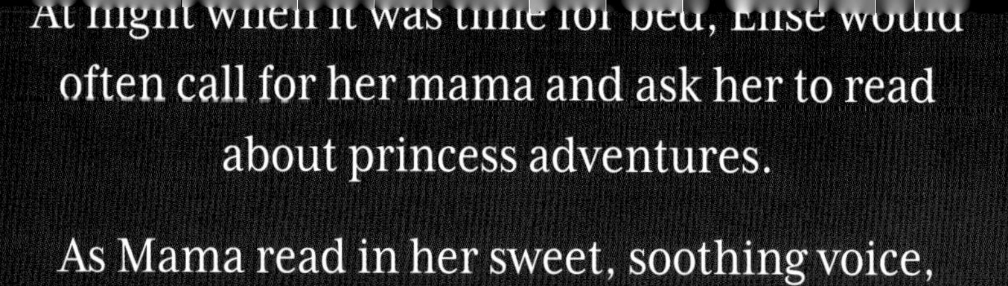

At night when it was time for bed, Elise would often call for her mama and ask her to read about princess adventures.

As Mama read in her sweet, soothing voice, Elise's eyes would light up as she imagined herself walking in a kingdom in her beautiful dress and sparkly crown, with a royal robe stretching behind her.

One night as her mama was tucking her in bed, Elise asked, "Does God really answer our prayers?"

"Yes, He does, sweet girl. Even when His answer is no, He knows what's best for us because He loves us. Now it's time to get your beauty sleep, my little princess."

"Just one more thing, Mama. Do you think God would answer my prayer to be a real princess?"

"Hmmm. Let's ask Him and see what happens."

And so Elise prayed a princess prayer:

"Dear God,

Thank you for my soft, cozy bed and for chocolate chip cookies. And God, will you please turn me into a real princess with a beautiful dress and sparkly crown with a long royal robe? Amen!"

The next morning, Elise leaped out of bed and began her search. She wanted to see if God had answered her prayer.

She opened her dress-up box. She saw her pretend crown and her sparkly costume dress and her brother's truck.

But they looked exactly the same.

Next, she looked in her closet.

Where are you, real crown?
Are you hanging up high, sparkly dress and royal robe?

But her closet looked just like it did yesterday.

After she put on her favorite outfit, Elise went outside and sat on her tire swing to think. "Now where should I look?" she said.

BELLA

Then Elise searched Bella's doghouse, just in case.

"Bella, what are you chewing on? If it's my real crown, it's made of pure gold, you know."

Bella barked, and the old shoe in her mouth dropped to the ground.

Maybe it takes awhile to make a sparkly dress just my size, Elise thought.

Elise prayed the princess prayer with her mama again that night. And then again on Tuesday, Wednesday, and every day for the rest of the week.

On Sunday, Elise went to church. Her teacher placed a gift bag in front of each child. She said, "Did you know that God is called the King of kings? And He sits on a throne in heaven? God loves you so much that He chose you to be His royal children . . . to be part of His real heavenly kingdom!"

Elise's eyes got really big. She asked, "Does that mean I am a real princess?"

"Yes, Elise. You are a real princess in God's kingdom!"

Everyone opened their little bags and found two crowns inside—one to wear and one to give to someone else, to share God's love. The crown sparkled, but Elise's smile sparkled more. She couldn't wait to tell her mama that God had answered her princess prayer!

When Mama arrived at the door to pick her up,
Elise ran to her arms and hugged her tight.
"Guess what, Mama? God made us both real
princesses in His kingdom!"
Then she pulled out the other crown and put it on her mama's head.

Tears welled up in her mama's eyes.

"What's wrong?" Elise asked, still hugging her tightly.
"Aren't you happy God answered my prayer?"

"Oh, Elise, these are happy tears! Because of your prayer, I just
realized that we both belong to the royal family of God."

They walked to the car holding hands and laughing as they admired each other's crowns, which were extra sparkly in the sunlight. Then Elise twirled around and said, "Thank you, God, for choosing me and my mama to be your princesses!"

A LETTER FROM MY KING

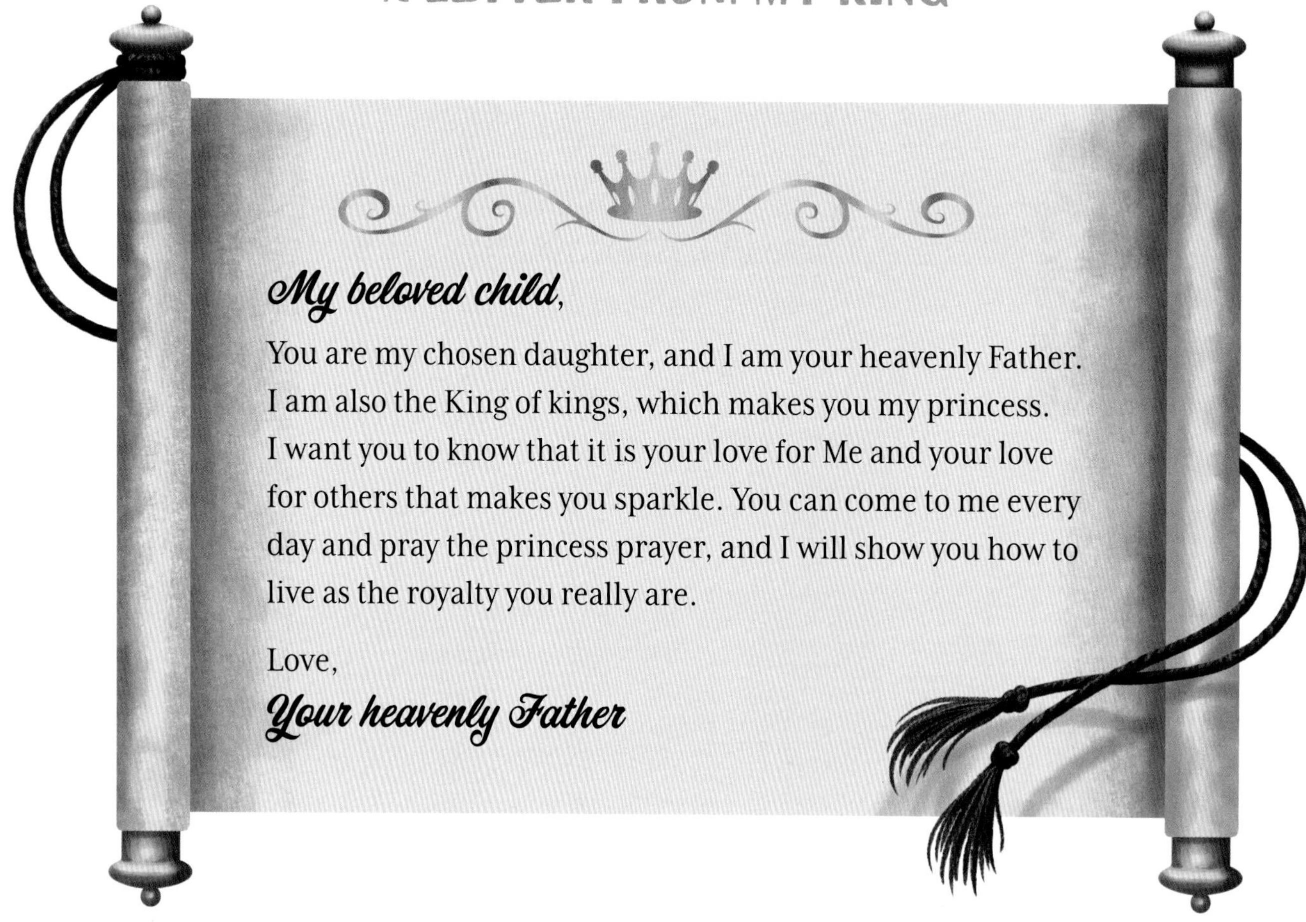

My beloved child,

You are my chosen daughter, and I am your heavenly Father. I am also the King of kings, which makes you my princess. I want you to know that it is your love for Me and your love for others that makes you sparkle. You can come to me every day and pray the princess prayer, and I will show you how to live as the royalty you really are.

Love,

Your heavenly Father

TREASURE OF TRUTH

"You didn't choose me. I chose you."

John 15:16